WHERE DRAGONS FLY

LAND OF STARS BOOK 1

HANNAH SPARKS

Illustrated by
KATHERINE NEWTON

Published by Hannah Ellis
www.authorhannahellis.com

ISBN: 978-3-948922-00-9 (Paperback)
ISBN: 978-3-948922-03-0 (Hardback)

Cover design and illustrations by Katherine Newton
www.kpunktnewton.com

For my boys, Lukas and Alex
who love stories about dragons!

CHAPTER ONE
SCHOOL HOLIDAYS

Until he was eight years old, Ethan Broom's life was very ordinary. He lived with his dad in a cosy little house on a quiet road just outside of the town. There were seven other houses on their road. Often, the children from those houses played together outside but Ethan never joined them. He didn't fit in well with the other kids.

Mr Broom, Ethan's dad, always left the house early to go to work. He was a street cleaner and spent all day driving around the town in a funny little orange car. Spiky brushes stuck out beside the wheels and spun around to sweep the dusty streets. Ethan's dad said it was good to work outside and to be able to stop and chat to people as he went. He came home early so he was always waiting when Ethan got home from school. Most other dads didn't get home until much later.

The only thing Ethan didn't like about his dad's job was that he had to work on Saturdays. That meant Ethan was alone all day. Mr Broom couldn't afford a babysitter and there wasn't any family nearby to look after Ethan.

Sunday was Ethan's favourite day. He'd spend the whole day with his dad. They'd play football in the back garden or get the bus into the countryside and walk through the forest, looking at the birds and paddling in the small stream.

What Ethan always dreaded were the school holidays. Most children love time off school. But most children spent the holidays playing with other kids or going on lovely holidays or being spoiled by grandparents. Not Ethan. For him, school holidays were like a whole load of Saturdays all stuck together. It was a lot of time alone. He'd always hated school holidays. But that was about to change.

On the first day of the summer holidays when Ethan was eight years old, he ate toast for breakfast with his dad. The thought of six long, boring weeks at home on his own felt awful. He tried to be brave, but his eyes tingled as though they might start crying all on their own.

"Maybe you could take some time off work?" he said, looking hopefully at his dad. "Then we could play together, or maybe we could go on a holiday? What if we took a train to the seaside? We could build sandcastles and swim in the sea." Ethan got excited just thinking about all the fun things they could do.

His dad tapped his fingers on the table with a sad glint in his eyes. "I'm sorry," he said. "I have to work."

They needed the money. Ethan knew that really.

"It's okay," Ethan said, trying to smile.

Mr Broom stood up and ruffled Ethan's brown hair. "Why don't you play outside with the other kids?"

"Maybe," he replied weakly. Ethan had tried to join them before but the other kids were all so confident and he never knew what to say. He didn't have cool toys like them either, and they laughed at him because his last name was Broom. They made silly jokes, saying he should be sweeping.

"What about Amelia?" his dad asked. "She's always on her own. I could ask her mum if she can come over here to play?"

"Don't do that," Ethan said quickly. "I'll go out later. I'm fine."

Amelia Hopton lived in the house across the road. She was in Ethan's class at school. Her hair was pitch-black and her skin was pale. The other kids called her a vampire. Ethan could see her house from his bedroom window and sometimes he'd see her sitting in her window reading a book.

If Ethan started playing with Amelia, he'd get teased even more. But she probably wouldn't want to play with him anyway.

"Will you be okay?" his dad asked.

"I'll be fine," Ethan said, trying his best to sound happy.

His dad's forehead wrinkled like it always did when he was worried or thinking a lot. He glanced at his watch and then back at Ethan, as though he didn't know whether to stay or go.

"I have something special for you to play with," he said in a rush, then walked out of the kitchen and hurried upstairs.

"What?" Ethan shouted. "What is it?"

"Wait a minute!" his dad called back. "You'll see."

E than went into the living room. He sat on the old brown couch, listening to the creak of the floorboards as his dad moved around upstairs.

"I've had these for a while," Mr Broom said when he came back down. He placed a small wooden box on the table. "They're very special so you have to look after them carefully."

"What is it?" Ethan leaned forward to get a better look at the box. It was quite plain except for a little padlock that held the latch firmly in place. The padlock was gold and shiny with a wonderful swirly pattern. "Where's the key?" Ethan asked.

Mr Broom held up a beautiful gold key. It had tiny red stones in the end of it, and they sparkled as the light caught them. Ethan ran his fingers over the key before hastily putting it into the lock. There was a small click as it unlocked. He peered inside.

He wrinkled his nose as he reached into the box. Something cold and hard pressed against his hand. He pulled it out and stared at it – a green dragon figure made from glass! It was smooth under his thumb. He looked back at the box and saw another dragon. That one was orange.

"What are they, Dad?"

"Dragons, of course!"

"But are they for a game?" Ethan asked.

"I don't really know."

Ethan turned the delicate dragon figure over in his hand. "Where did they come from?"

"I found them when I was working," Mr Broom said. "Sitting beside a dustbin as though they were waiting for me."

"And you just took them?" Ethan didn't like it when his dad found things on the streets and brought them home. He wished he would buy him toys from the shops like the other parents did.

"There was a note with it," his dad said.

"What did it say?" Ethan asked.

Mr Broom held out a crumpled piece of paper with the words:

Caution! Box contains magic.

"That was really with it?" Ethan wasn't sure if his dad was telling stories to cheer him up.

"Yes."

It was a bit disappointing, Ethan thought. Because there wasn't any magic in the box; just someone's dusty old dragon figures.

"I thought they might be fun for you to play with while I'm at work," his dad said.

Ethan wasn't sure how the little pieces would

keep him entertained all day. In fact, he wasn't even sure how he was supposed to play with them. He'd never been very good at playing make-believe.

"Thanks, Dad," he said.

"Be careful, though." His dad winked at him. "They're full of magic. You never know what might happen!"

CHAPTER THREE
HOME ALONE

After his dad left for work, Ethan soon got bored. He stared at the dragon figures for a while and then left them on the living room table and went up to his room. Flopping onto his bed, he flicked through a comic book.

The sound of children playing drifted up to his room. When he walked to the window, he saw kids playing on bikes and skateboards and scooters. They were laughing and shouting to each other as they played.

If only he was brave enough to go out and talk to them and join their games.

He was about to move away from the window when he caught sight of Amelia Hopton. She was sitting in her window in the house across the road. There was a book in her hand but she wasn't looking at it. She was staring at Ethan. Quickly, he whipped his gaze away. It made him uncomfortable the way she looked at him. She didn't smile or wave, just stared.

Ethan moved from the window. It wasn't lunchtime yet but he was starting to feel hungry. Down in the kitchen, he ate the sandwich his dad had left out for him. He got himself a drink of water and then went to the living room. Without thinking, he lifted the small green dragon figure up from the table and traced a finger over the smooth glass.

The children's laughter coming from outside pulled him like a magnet and he found himself looking out of the front window. He really wanted to go out and play. If he had cool toys like the other kids it would be so much easier.

Suddenly, he began to feel angry. He was angry with his dad for not buying him a bike. And for working all summer and leaving him alone.

A ball bounced into the front garden. Ethan didn't have chance to move out of sight before a boy came into the garden looking for it. His name was Freddie and he was a year older than Ethan. Freddie was mean and loud.

When Freddie saw Ethan, he sneered at him through the window.

"Hey, Broom!" he called. "Shouldn't you be cleaning?"

Tears filled Ethan's eyes until he couldn't see properly anymore. All he was aware of was the sound of Freddie laughing. Ethan didn't realise he was squeezing the little dragon in his hand. His hand formed a tight fist until the tail of the dragon dug into his palm.

Ethan looked down. But it was too late.

He felt himself falling.

CHAPTER FOUR
A DRAGON

E than felt as though the floor had fallen from beneath him. He wanted to scream but he couldn't catch his breath. His head seemed to spin and he was dizzy. Bright colours swirled around him. A strong wind blew, and everything turned bright blue. It felt like he was flying. When he saw fluffy white clouds, he realised he *was* flying.

"Hold tight," a rumbling voice said.

Ethan looked down. He was sitting on something green and scaly. When he glanced to the side, he saw huge green wings spread out. Ethan thought he must be dreaming. Except it didn't feel like a dream. It felt very real.

There was a rumble in the sky, like thunder. It took Ethan a moment to realise it wasn't thunder at all; it was laughter. Terrified he was going to fall, Ethan clung onto the scaly green neck that stretched out in from of him. Then the neck moved, and he came face to face with the head of a dragon. It couldn't be though. Dragons weren't real.

The dragon's eyes were bright green and glowed with tiny flecks of gold. Smoke puffed from his nose when he laughed.

"Hold tight!" the dragon said again before he turned and reached his head high up into the sky. They flew faster and Ethan held on tightly as they disappeared into a huge white cloud. The wind whipped at his face and finally he opened his mouth and let out an almighty scream. Ethan's lungs rattled in his chest. He'd never screamed so hard in all his life. The noise burst out of him and mixed with the sound of the dragon's laughter.

When they erupted out above the cloud, Ethan looked down. The fluffy clouds below him were like a wonderful soft blanket. His screaming faded and the dragon slowed. Ethan still clung on tightly. He kept telling himself it must be a dream and he'd wake up any minute.

The dragon moved slowly down through the clouds until they were gliding over a lush green forest.

"Where is it?" the low voice said.

Surely the dragon wasn't talking to Ethan? And if he was, what was he looking for?

"What's that, down there?" Ethan whispered. There was a break in the trees below and in the middle of the clearing was a huge letter H.

"Here we are!" the dragon said, flying straight at the H. He landed on the ground right in the middle of it. Up close, Ethan saw that the H was made from bright orange flowers, growing in a perfect pattern.

He slid from the dragon's back as they landed on solid ground. The delicate flowers, which had been squashed by the heavy dragon, sprang back up as soon as he moved away from them.

The forest was thick with trees and Ethan was worried he'd get lost if he ran away. That was what he should be doing though. When there was a dragon standing right in front of you, you should definitely run. That's what a sensible person would do.

All Ethan could do was sit and stare at the green creature in front of him. Then, just as he thought he couldn't be any more scared, the ground began to shake.

CHAPTER FIVE
WHERE AM I?

Ethan watched as the dragon jumped up and down. He flapped his wings, causing so much wind that leaves fell from the trees and pine needles jiggled beside Ethan making it look as though the ground was moving . It was scary at first but when he saw how happy the dragon looked, Ethan wasn't as frightened.

"Please could you stop that?" he said loudly.

The dragon stopped his jumping. "Sorry," he said in his low voice. "I'm excited. It's a long time since I've made the flight to your world. We haven't had a child to visit in ages."

Ethan ducked his head as the dragon stretched. He wiggled his shoulders, causing another huge gust of wind as his wings flapped.

"Please could you stop that too?" Ethan asked, smoothing his hair back into place.

The dragon groaned. "It's so nice to stretch my wings. I slept for far too long." He turned and stared at Ethan. Then he moved his face down until it was right in front of Ethan's. His breath was hot, and Ethan scrambled backwards.

"What's your name?" the dragon asked.

"I'm Ethan." He scrabbled to stand up. "Who are you?"

"I'm Enzo." The dragon smiled widely and suddenly he didn't seem frightening at all. With his wings folded at his sides, he didn't seem as big. The top of Ethan's head came about halfway up the dragon's body. The round nostrils at the end of his snout grew and shrank as he breathed.

"Y– You're a dragon?" Ethan stuttered, finding it hard to believe his eyes.

"Of course." Enzo laughed, making his whole body shake.

"I didn't think dragons were real," Ethan said quietly.

"Oh, dragons are very real. Touch me!" Slowly, he stretched out his front leg.

Ethan ran his fingers over the scales. They

looked hard but were quite squishy really. He'd been too scared to notice when he was flying on the dragon.

Enzo laughed his low, rumbly laugh, "That tickles."

"Where are we?" Ethan asked as he turned to look around. All he could see were trees.

"Here!" Enzo said. "Didn't you see the sign?" He pointed a claw at the orange flowers.

"It looked like the place where helicopters land," Ethan said.

"Helicopters?" Enzo chuckled. "I hope not."

"What's the H for then?"

"*Here*, of course."

"I don't understand," Ethan said.

Enzo looked up. "When I'm flying over the trees, it's hard to find a place to land. The H tells me exactly where. Right *here*!"

"That's silly." Ethan had almost forgotten to be scared. And suddenly it didn't even feel that strange that he was talking to a dragon.

"It makes perfect sense to me," Enzo said. "Come on. Let's go."

"Where are we going?" Ethan hurried to catch up as Enzo set off walking into the forest.

"To see a friend of mine," Enzo said. "Pascal always likes it when children come to visit. He'll probably want you to help him with something."

Ethan's eyes widened. "Is Pascal another dragon?"

"No." Enzo's eyes sparkled when he turned his head to Ethan. "Pascal is a penguin."

CHAPTER SIX
PASCAL THE PENGUIN

A penguin? Had Ethan heard right? There couldn't really be a penguin in a forest. And dragons weren't usually friends with penguins, were they? But, earlier that same day, Ethan hadn't even believed in dragons. Now he was following one through a forest to visit a penguin!

They walked for about five minutes before they emerged from the forest and arrived at the edge of a field. It was bare except for a little house at the far side. Amazingly, the house was covered in thick snow. In fact, the whole area around the house was white with snow and ice. Icicles hung from the roof. It was as though someone had cut out a winter scene and dropped it on a patch of green grass. They walked across the field, stopping where the grass met the snow.

"Who's there?" a small voice asked. It belonged to a penguin standing in the doorway of the icy house. He had a bright red scarf around his neck and a bobble hat on his head. A pair of glasses hung on a chain around his neck.

"Pascal!" Enzo's excited voice boomed all around.

"Is that you, Enzo?" The penguin wobbled from side to side as he ventured down the slippery path towards them. He squinted up at the dragon when he got near. "Oh, yes!" he beamed. "Don't come too close. I don't want your hot breath melting my house."

"Put your glasses on," Enzo chuckled. "What good are glasses if they're not on your face?"

"They fell off." Pascal turned his head quickly from side to side and waved a flipper around. The end of his flipper didn't reach up to his face so he couldn't get the glasses back on.

"Let me help," Enzo said.

"No!" the penguin shouted, then took a few wobbly steps backwards. "Don't come near me with those claws! You'll take an eye out."

"Shall I help?" Ethan asked quietly.

"Aaarggh!" the penguin shrieked and jumped in fright.

"Calm down," Enzo said. "This is my friend, Ethan."

"You've brought another child!" The penguin flapped his wings against his sides excitedly. "You haven't brought a child in so long."

"No one's been playing with the glass dragons," Enzo said. "But now Ethan's here!"

Ethan was confused. Did Enzo mean the glass dragons his dad had given him? Was that why he was there?

The penguin made a funny clicking sound. "I can't see well without my glasses."

Slowly, Ethan moved towards the penguin and reached for his glasses. Then carefully pushed them onto Pascal's face and balanced them on his tiny orange beak. The penguin came up to Ethan's shoulder. Ethan was quite short for his age and wasn't used to being taller than anyone.

The penguin blinked. His eyes were magnified by his thick glasses and looked quite funny.

"Hello!" he said to Ethan. "I'm Pascal. How wonderful to meet you."

When he held out a flipper, Ethan shook it politely. If felt a little rubbery but not at all wet, as Ethan had expected.

"I'm so glad you're here," Pascal said. "Children are always so helpful. I wonder if you could help me." He shook his head and smiled. "I'm being very rude. First, I'll show you around. Have you seen our wonderful sky?"

CHAPTER SEVEN
STARS IN DAYLIGHT

When he'd been in the forest, Ethan hadn't been able to see the sky because of all the trees. Now he tipped his head back to look at the spectacular sight above.

The sky was bright blue. The kind of sky you get on a wonderfully sunny day right in the middle of summer. Except there was no sun. Instead, the sky sparkled with stars. It was bright light and the middle of the day. But the sky was full of stars. Not just normal silver stars either, but all different colours. Imagine someone threw a jar of multicoloured glitter into a bright blue sky and it stuck there. That's what this sky looked like.

"It's the most amazing sky I've ever seen," Ethan said. "There are so many stars."

Pascal chuckled. "The sky's only half full now. You should see it when it's completely full."

"What do you mean?" Ethan asked.

"More stars appear every day," Enzo explained. "Until it's full."

"And then what happens?" Ethan asked.

"It empties, of course," Pascal replied.

Ethan blinked and stared up at the beautiful twinkling sky. He didn't quite understand.

"So, what do you think of Steorra?" Pascal asked.

Ethan was so confused. "What's Steorra?"

"Not *what*," Pascal said. "*Where!* This is

Steorra." He held his flipper out and turned quickly, gesturing to everything around.

"Do you live here alone?" Ethan asked. There only seemed to be one house and he'd feel very sorry for Pascal if he lived there all alone.

"Oh, no!" Pascal looked around him. "The view from here isn't great. Come on, follow me…" He turned and waddled towards the house.

Ethan stared up at Enzo who gave him a little nudge. "Go on," he said. "It's alright."

"Don't you come, Enzo!" Pascal called back. "You'll melt my house."

"I'm waiting right here," Enzo said cheerfully. He lowered himself down to lay on the grass.

Ethan felt a bit nervous as he followed the penguin. He almost lost his footing when he stepped from the green grass onto the icy path. After a moment he found it was best to shuffle his feet rather than walk normally. When they reached the front door, Ethan saw it wasn't a door at all, just an icy archway. And the house wasn't made from bricks like a normal house, but from blocks of ice.

"It's so cold." Ethan's teeth began to chatter

as he ducked his head under the archway and stepped inside.

"Here." Pascal gave him a blue hat and scarf, and he put them on as fast as he could. "Upstairs!" Pascal said.

Ethan's eyes felt as though they might fall out of his head when he looked at the stairs. It wasn't an ordinary staircase. Penguins didn't have proper legs, so of course a normal staircase wouldn't be any good. The square blocks of ice looked like stairs, except that they were moving. It was like an escalator made of ice. Pascal did a little hop up onto a moving block.

"Jump on!" he called behind him.

Ethan stepped onto a block of ice. It carried him steadily up to the top part of the house. For a moment, Ethan wondered how they'd get down again since the escalator was only going up. Then he saw the icy slide which ran beside the stairs. It looked like it would be a fast way down.

At the top of the stairs, Pascal was flapping a flipper, indicating that Ethan should follow him.

"Is that your bed?" Ethan asked, pointing to a slab of ice in the room they came to. There was a penguin-shaped dip in the middle of the rectangular block.

"Yes," Pascal said. "But never mind that. Come and look at the view."

Slowly and carefully, Ethan walked over to the window - it was just a hole in the frozen wall.

"Wow!" Ethan whispered as he stared outside. The view was much better from up there.

CHAPTER EIGHT
LEMONADE OR ORANGE JUICE

"Almost everyone lives down in the village," Pascal said, pointing a flipper. "I like it up here where it's quieter."

Ethan stared out of the window into the valley below. It took a moment for his eyes to get used to the brightness. As he blinked, his eyes focussed and he saw a lake with little houses beside it. They appeared to be made from ice like Pascal's. Mountains loomed in the distance but the town down below seemed to sparkle and glow. The glittery light of the stars reflected on the surface of the lake and on the ice and snow on the ground.

"It's so beautiful," Ethan said. "Are there more penguins down there?"

"Lots of penguins," Pascal said. "And goblins, fairies, pixies, a polar bear or two..."

"Can they all speak?" Ethan asked.

"Of course they can all speak!" Pascal smiled and began to waddle out of the room. "Come on. I'd like to go down to the village."

At the top of the stairs, Pascal plopped onto his tummy and set off down the slide beside the ice escalator. He whizzed all the way down and shot out of the front door. When he disappeared, Ethan carefully sat at the top.

Maybe if he pushed his feet into the ice he wouldn't go so fast. But when he eased himself over the edge, his feet couldn't get a grip on the ice. Closing his eyes tight, he gasped and grabbed at the ice with his hands.

It made no difference and he whizzed faster and faster down the ramp, feeling completely out of control. When he shot out of the door and onto the front path, he began to slow down. Finally he came to a stop in front of Enzo and Pascal. Now that he'd made it safely down, he felt a rush of excitement at the ride.

"That was brilliant!" he said.

Enzo yawned as he stood up. "I was having a little nap."

"Now that you're awake we'll go down to the village," Pascal said.

It looked a long way down into the village and Ethan was starting to worry about getting home. He shouldn't really go walking around strange villages. And what if everyone wasn't as friendly as Enzo and Pascal?

"I– I think maybe I should go home soon," Ethan stuttered.

"We've still got time," Enzo said. "I'll get you home on time, don't worry."

"But what if my dad comes home and I'm not there?" Ethan asked.

"You won't be late," Pascal reassured him. "How about we have a drink before we go into the village? I can tell you what I need help with."

Pascal waddled off the ice and onto the grass. "Do you prefer orange juice or lemonade?" he called over his shoulder.

At home, Ethan only drank water, so lemonade or orange juice sounded like quite a treat. It made him forget his worries about getting home.

"Lemonade," he said and began to follow Pascal. "But where are we going?"

"You'll see," Pascal said.

When Enzo set off walking, the ground seemed to shake a little.

"Walk softly!" Pascal said with a smile.

"Sorry." Enzo sprang up into the air and opened his wings. Then he flew across the field. He stopped a little way ahead, beside two trees at the edge of the field. Beyond the trees was the steep slope down to the village.

Ethan was very confused when they caught up to Enzo. Where on earth were they going to get a drink from? Before he could ask, he noticed the trees were bursting with fruit.

One tree was filled with juicy ripe oranges. The other was a lemon tree with hundreds of lemons hanging on the branches.

"Are we going to make lemonade?" Ethan asked, looking up at the pretty tree.

Enzo laughed, making the leaves on the trees shake.

"We don't have to make it," Pascal said, pointing a flipper to the tree trunk. A tap stuck out of it. It looked just like the outdoor tap at the back of Ethan's house.

Ethan moved closer, wondering if it was possible that lemonade would come out of the tap.

There was only one way to find out.

CHAPTER NINE
TIME TO GO

Beside the tree were small cups made from wood. Ethan took one and held it under the tap. Then he slowly turned the handle and watched in amazement as the yellow liquid filled his cup. It smelled sweet and delicious. When he took a sip, it tasted better than anything Ethan had ever tasted. He finished the lemonade in a few long gulps, then looked at Pascal.

"Can I try the orange juice too?" he asked.

"Have as much as you want," Pascal said. "It's not going to run out."

"Really?" Ethan put his cup under the tap on the trunk of the orange tree and watched the golden juice flow into it. "There's always more?" It was hard to imagine being able to drink orange juice or lemonade whenever you wanted.

"Yes," Pascal replied.

Ethan took his orange juice and sat down in the grass. The village was way down below and the colourful stars twinkled overhead. It was the most beautiful place he'd ever seen. Everything seemed to glow beneath the bright blue sky and the shiny stars. Ethan could just see the houses in the village. He felt a million miles away from home and the kids in his street.

Ethan was lost in thought when a butterfly fluttered in front of his face. It landed on his knee. When it turned to look at Ethan, he got a big shock.

"Hello!" the butterfly said, smiling at him. It had a face. A tiny face, of course, but it had eyes and a nose and a mouth - just like a person.

"Hello," Ethan said in a squeaky voice. He didn't mean to, but in his surprise, he stretched his leg out. It frightened the poor butterfly away. "Even the butterflies talk!"

"Of course," Pascal laughed. "What kind of creatures can't talk?"

"All of them," Ethan said. "At least where I live."

"I forgot things are different in your world," Pascal said. "It's a while since we've had any children here."

"Other children have been here?" Ethan asked.

"Yes." Pascal tapped his feet happily. "Very helpful they are too. Which reminds me. I need your help."

"With what?"

"I need you to help me find my fishing rod."

Enzo laughed loudly. "Is that all? You've lost your fishing rod?"

"I didn't lose it!" Pascal wobbled from side to side and his cheeks turned pink. He looked very angry. "Jojo took it!"

Enzo's smile disappeared and a puff of smoke shot out of his nostrils.

"Who's Jojo?" Ethan asked, starting to feel nervous again. Maybe there were giants or monsters in Steorra.

"Jojo is a fairy," Enzo said.

"A fairy?" That didn't sound very scary.

"Jojo's always up to mischief," Pascal said. "I think she flew away with my fishing rod when I wasn't looking. When I asked her about it she laughed and said she hadn't seen it but I'm sure she knows really."

"I bet she does," Enzo agreed. "It sounds like something Jojo would do."

"I can't catch fish," Pascal said. "Every day I have to ask another penguin to catch one for me."

"Can't you borrow one of their fishing rods?" Ethan asked.

Pascal's eyes blinked quickly. "The other penguins don't have fishing rods. They dive to catch fish."

"Can't you do that?"

"No!" Pascal said, looking a little upset. "I can't swim very well," he said quietly.

"Oh," Ethan said.

"So, will you help me look for it?" Pascal asked hopefully. "Children have better eyes than penguins. I'm sure it will be somewhere in the village."

"Okay," Ethan said. He was feeling much braver and really wanted to see the village. It would be great if he could help Pascal find his fishing rod too.

"I don't think we have time now," Enzo said. "We need to get you back before your dad gets home."

"Time always goes fast when we have visitors," Pascal said.

Ethan felt sad as he followed Enzo and Pascal back across the field. He really wanted to see the village.

"Maybe you can help next time you come," Pascal said as he waddled along.

"Next time?" Ethan peered up at Enzo. "I can come back again?"

"Whenever you want," Enzo told him.

"But how? I don't even know how I got here." Ethan thought back. The last thing he remembered at home was looking out of the window. And then a sharp prick in the palm of his hand. He'd been holding one of the dragon figures that his dad had given him. The green dragon. He looked up at Enzo. The dragon figure he'd been holding was the same colour as Enzo.

"You have the glass dragons, don't you?" Enzo asked.

"Yes." Ethan hurried to keep up. "Is that how I got here? They really are magic?"

Enzo's laughter filled the air. "The little dragons are full to the brim with magic."

CHAPTER TEN
BACK HOME

Outside Pascal's house, Ethan returned the scarf and hat. As Ethan and Enzo walked back to the forest, the little penguin stood in front of the house, flapping a wing. Ethan turned to wave one last time.

They walked quickly through the forest and soon arrived at the big orange H.

"*Here* we are!" Enzo said with a grin.

Ethan laughed. Maybe it did make sense.

"Ready to go?" Enzo asked.

Ethan looked around him. "Can I really come back again?" he asked.

Enzo nodded excitedly. "Just use the glass dragons."

"How do they work?" Ethan asked.

"You should know," he said with a smile. "You already got here once."

Ethan thought back to the moments before he'd found himself on Enzo's back, flying through the air. He'd been looking out of the living room window at Freddie.

"I was scared," Ethan said. "And I squeezed the glass dragon, then I was on your back."

Enzo smiled gently. "You wanted to be somewhere else, so it took you somewhere else. Now, let's go. I'm getting worried I won't get you home on time." He bent low to the ground, as though he was about to spring up into the air.

With a deep breath, Ethan stepped onto Enzo's bent knee and pulled himself up onto his back. "What happens to you when I leave?" Ethan asked, filled with curiosity. "Where do you live?"

"In a cave in the mountains at the other side of Steorra. Dragons sleep a lot, you know. Sometimes for months at a time. I feel like a nap now actually. Let's get you home. Hold tight!" Enzo called.

Ethan leaned forward and gripped Enzo's neck. He squeezed his eyes closed. A moment later he felt a whoosh of air as they took off. When he opened his eyes, they were high above the fluffy clouds. His eyelids clamped shut again and then he slowly opened one eye, just halfway.

When they swooped back down below the clouds, wonderful colours began to swirl all around. Ethan felt dizzy for a moment, and then everything stopped. He was standing in his living room in the exact spot he'd been before his adventure.

A noise at the front door made him turn his head.

"Hello!" his dad called.

Ethan ran into the hallway, surprised that his dad was home already. "What are you doing home so soon?" he asked.

"What do you mean?" His dad kicked off his grubby old boots. He checked his watch. "It's nearly dinner time. How was your day?" When he went to the kitchen, Ethan followed him. It didn't feel like the whole day had gone by.

"It was fine," Ethan said.

"What have you been doing?"

Ethan blinked quickly. "I– Er–" He looked down at his hand. The green dragon was still wrapped in his fist. "I played with the dragon," he said.

"I thought you'd like them." His dad opened the fridge and peered inside. "It's great for your imagination."

"Yes." Ethan's trip to Steorra seemed so real, but maybe it had all just been his imagination.

"What do you want for dinner?" his dad asked. "Fish fingers and chips?"

"Okay." Ethan took a seat at the kitchen table. The fish fingers made him think of Pascal and his missing fishing rod. He hoped Enzo was right and he could return to Steorra. The holidays wouldn't be at all boring if he could visit Pascal and Enzo every day. He could help find Pascal's fishing rod and explore the village. Maybe he'd make friends with more of the animals.

"I just saw Amelia's mum," his dad said. "She told me Amelia's already bored of the school holidays. Her mum's worried she'll spend the summer sitting in her window with her head in a book. So, I invited her to come over and play with you tomorrow. That'll be nice, won't it?"

"What?" Ethan had been quite happy thinking about Steorra. Why did his dad have to remind him of the boring school holidays and the kids who didn't want to be friends with him?

He was sure Amelia didn't really want to play with him either. Like Ethan, she never played with the other kids, but unlike him, it wasn't because she was scared to join their games. Once, when Ethan had heard someone call her a vampire because of her pale skin, Amelia had bared her teeth and hissed at them. Then laughed as she walked away.

"I don't want her to come here," Ethan complained.

"I already said she could. It'll be good for you to have company."

Ethan wanted to say that he had plenty of company. But he couldn't tell his dad about Enzo and Pascal. Why on earth had his dad invited Amelia over? For once Ethan was excited about the holidays. He wanted to go on another adventure in Steorra.

But he couldn't do that with Amelia around.

CHAPTER ELEVEN
AMELIA HOPTON

It was the middle of the next morning when the knock came at the front door. Ethan let out a sigh when he stood up from the couch. He really wished his dad hadn't invited Amelia over. He didn't want to play with a girl and had no idea what he would talk to her about.

He forced himself to smile when he opened the door. Amelia was standing beside her mum, looking down at her feet. Her mum had a hand on Amelia's shoulder as though she'd dragged her from their house and was now keeping hold of her so she didn't run away.

"Hi!" Amelia's mum said cheerily. "Amelia's so excited about spending the day with you."

That was weird because Amelia definitely

didn't look excited. Ethan kept smiling; he didn't know what to say.

"Amelia's brought some games," her mum said, shoving a backpack into Amelia's arms and giving her a gentle push. "I made you both sandwiches too." She held out a Tupperware box and Ethan took it from her.

"Thanks," he mumbled.

"I'm sure you'll have a great time together," she said. Then she turned and walked back to the road. "See you later!"

As Ethan watched her go, he noticed the kids playing outside again. They called out to each other as they rode along the pavement on their bikes. Ethan no longer cared about not having a bike. Not now he had his glass dragons. They were safely up in his room while Amelia was there, but tomorrow he was definitely going on another adventure.

Amelia stood in the hallway, clutching her backpack and staring at the wall.

"What games have you got?" Ethan asked.

She sighed and rolled her eyes. "Junior Scrabble, Junior Monopoly, Boggle and a pack of cards."

Ethan went into the living room and she followed. He didn't like the way she gazed around the room. It was quite dull and drab. Amelia's house was probably lovely and bright. It was definitely much bigger than their house.

"What do you want to play first?" he asked.

"I don't care," she said. "I brought my book too. I'd rather read. Can I see your bedroom? From the window you can see my bedroom, can't you?"

Ethan panicked. He didn't want her to go upstairs and find the dragons. "Why don't we play Scrabble?" he said quickly.

"Okay." Amelia sat heavily on the couch and began to get the game out of the bag.

"I'll just put the sandwiches in the kitchen," Ethan said.

He was only in the kitchen for a moment, but when he came back to the living room, Amelia had gone. Turning in a circle, he looked around as though maybe he'd just missed her. Then he heard the floorboards creaking above his head. He hurried to the stairs. Why was she snooping? It was annoying enough having her around for the day, without having to make sure she wasn't going through his things.

He found her in his bedroom. The little wooden box was open beside her.

"What are you doing?" he asked, striding

over and looking into the box. The green dragon was there but the orange one was missing. Ethan noticed Amelia's left hand was balled into a fist. The orange tail of the dragon was just peeking out between her fingers. He tried not to worry. After all, the magic only worked when you wished you were somewhere else.

"Give me that back!" Ethan said, stepping forward to take the dragon.

Amelia gave him a puzzled look.

Then, she vanished.

CHAPTER TWELVE
FLYING WITH AMELIA

The high-pitched screaming made Ethan's ears hurt. As soon as Amelia disappeared, Ethan had reached into the box. He picked up the green dragon and squeezed hard, wishing he was back in Steorra.

In an instant, he felt Enzo's scaly back beneath him and clung on for dear life. When he braved opening his eyes, he saw the fiery orange dragon beside him. Amelia was screaming, just like Ethan had done when he'd found himself unexpectedly flying on a dragon.

"It's okay," Ethan called out, trying to reassure her.

"It's more than okay!" she shouted back. "It's AMAZING!"

Ethan blinked a couple of times and realised

she hadn't been screaming in fright, as he had, but squealing and screeching in excitement. What on earth was wrong with her? Why wasn't she terrified?

"Hold on tight!" Ethan said as Amelia sat up straight and flung her arms out to the sides. Was she completely crazy?

"What's happening?" she shouted into the wind.

"Erm... We're flying on dragons," Ethan called.

"That's what I thought." Amelia threw her head back and laughed loudly. "Am I dreaming?"

"I don't think so," Ethan said. "You need to hold on."

Amelia leaned forward, running her hands along the scales of the dragon's neck. "Faster!" she called.

Ethan's eyes widened.

"Faster!" Amelia said again, louder this time.

The orange dragon turned its head slightly and seemed to smile at Enzo. Ethan's stomach felt funny as the dragons extended their necks and soared into the clouds. They seemed to be racing.

Amelia howled like a wolf and then shook

her head so her black hair flew wildly out behind her. All Ethan could do was cling on and hope he didn't fall. It seemed to take ages before the two dragons slowed. They descended through the clouds and flew low over the forest.

"Here!" Ethan called out when he spotted the landing site.

They glided down and landed gracefully in the clearing.

Again, Ethan stayed low to the ground after he rolled clumsily off Enzo's back. This time there were two dragons jumping around, and more leaves and pine needles rained down from the trees.

Amelia jumped around with the dragons, throwing her arms in the air and cheering wildly.

"Weren't you scared?" Ethan asked when the dragons calmed down.

"Why would I be scared?" Amelia's green eyes were wide and filled with wonder. She walked up and down beside the orange dragon. "My whole life I've dreamed of riding on a dragon, and today I actually got to do it." She stroked the dragon's leg. "Thank you," she said.

"You're welcome." The orange dragon was the same size as Enzo but spoke much more softly. "And thank *you*," she said, bowing her head so her piercing orange eyes were level with Amelia's. "It's so good to stretch my wings. The flight to your world is always fun. I'm Erla, by the way. That's Enzo. What's your name?"

"I'm Amelia!" she said, then spun around to face Ethan. "I thought today was going to be the most boring day ever, but it's turned out to be the best. Why didn't you tell me you had magical dragons?"

Ethan frowned. "I wasn't sure anyone would believe me."

"Well, I believe it." She grinned and looked around. "We're going to have the greatest adventure of all time!"

CHAPTER THIRTEEN
AMELIA MEETS PASCAL

"Where are we?" Amelia asked as they set off walking through the forest.

"It's called Steorra," Ethan told her.

"Wow!" Amelia gasped. "That sounds magical."

Erla ducked underneath a low tree branch. "It means land of stars."

Amelia immediately tipped her head back to look up.

"We need to get out from under the trees," Ethan told her. "Then you'll see the sky. It's filled with stars even in daylight."

"It's so exciting," Amelia said, walking faster as the edge of the forest came into view.

Enzo let out a low chuckle. "You're not scared at all, are you?"

"Why would I be scared?" Amelia asked. "You're not going to eat us, are you?"

Enzo laughed so loudly the trees shook and pine needles fell around them. "Not unless we get *really* hungry."

"I didn't think so," Amelia said. "You look like kind dragons. Nothing bad can happen when you've got friendly dragons with you." She turned back to Ethan. "Come on! Hurry up. I'll bet there's loads to explore."

Ethan wondered why the magic in the glass dragons had worked for Amelia. He'd thought it only worked if you wished you were somewhere else. Maybe Amelia hadn't wanted to be at his house. It made him feel strange to think she'd wished she didn't have to spend the day with him.

When they walked out of the forest, Amelia stared up at the stars. She only snatched her gaze away when Pascal called out to them.

"Who's there?" he shouted, flapping and waddling in his doorway.

"A talking penguin?" Amelia said with delight. "This is incredible!"

Ethan met Pascal halfway down the icy path and pushed his glasses on for him. He blinked up at him.

"Oh, you're back! Lovely to see you again, Ethan." He glanced at the dragons. "Stay away!" he said to them. "Don't melt my house with your hot breath."

After introducing Amelia to Pascal, Ethan asked if he could show her the house. He didn't feel nervous like he had the previous day. Showing Amelia around was great fun - her eyes were wide with wonder when she saw the moving ice staircase.

"Come on." Ethan hopped on and beckoned for her to follow.

Amelia didn't stand still on the ice blocks, and almost knocked Ethan over as she raced past him. At the top, she didn't stop but let out a cry of delight as she jumped straight onto the slide. She didn't sit as Ethan had done but stood and slid all the way down on her feet. Somehow, she managed to stop at the bottom and gave another whoop of joy. Then she rushed up the stairs again to join Ethan.

"Come and look at the view," he said, grinning at her enthusiasm.

She bounded into the little bedroom ahead of Ethan and stood in the window. Finally, she was quiet. Her eyes drifted up to the starry sky, and then down to the village at the bottom of the steep grassy hill.

"Can we go down there?" she asked.

"I haven't been into the village yet," Ethan said. "I think we can. We just need to make sure we get home before my dad gets back."

"Are you serious?" Amelia turned to face Ethan. "We're on a magical adventure and you're thinking about getting home on time? I want to explore. We have to go and see what's down the hill."

"I promised I'd help Pascal find his fishing

rod," Ethan said. "He thinks it's in the village somewhere."

"Great! It's like a treasure hunt!"

Amelia rushed out of the bedroom and slid back downstairs on her feet. Cautiously, Ethan sat down at the top of the slide. He whizzed all the way out through the doorway and along the slippery path. When he came to a stop he had a huge smile on his face.

"We want to go down the hill," Amelia told Pascal and the dragons. "Can we go now?"

Enzo smiled. "Yes. We should see if we can find Jojo and ask her about the missing fishing rod."

"Who's Jojo?" Amelia asked.

"A fairy," Pascal said, shaking his head. "A very troublesome fairy."

"A fairy!" Amelia jumped up and down, clapping her hands together. "What are we waiting for? Let's go!"

At the top of the grassy hill, Pascal didn't stop and wait; he leaned forwards until he toppled onto his belly.

"See you at the bottom," he called as he shot off down the steep slope.

"That looks like fun!" Amelia said.

"We can't slide down like that," Ethan said quickly. "It's dangerous."

Erla appeared beside them with what seemed to be a tree trunk in her claws. When she dropped it into the short grass beside them, Ethan saw the hollowed out middle. It looked as though it had come from a log flume ride.

"Brilliant!" Amelia shouted and jumped straight in.

"That's going to go really fast," Ethan said,

looking down the hillside. He could just make out Pascal at the bottom.

"Come on!" Amelia grabbed at his hand and Ethan reluctantly climbed into the tree trunk behind her.

"Ready?" Enzo said.

Ethan opened his mouth to say he wasn't quite ready and he wasn't sure it was a good idea at all. But it was too late; Enzo had already given them a gentle nudge over the edge.

Ethan grabbed hold of the side of the tree as they picked up speed. Amelia's jet-black hair whipped into his face and all he could see were black strands mixed with green flecks of grass which shot up all around them. Amelia threw her head back and howled like a wolf again.

"How are we going to stop?" Ethan cried.

Amelia didn't seem to care about that as she let out squeals of joy. She was painfully loud. Eventually, the ground levelled out and the tree trunk slowed. Pushing Amelia's hair from his face, Ethan blinked the village into view. There were some stone cottages with roofs made from sticks. At the far side of the village, the houses seemed to be snow-covered, like Pascal's.

Finally, they came to a dead stop quite close to the first house.

"What's that?" Amelia said in a high-pitched voice as she climbed out of the tree trunk.

"A polar bear," Ethan said. He was amazed at how calm he sounded.

The enormous white bear was quite close to them. Ethan had read about how vicious polar bears could be. For some reason, he wasn't particularly scared as he stood beside Amelia. Maybe Amelia's bravery was rubbing off on him.

Or maybe it was because the polar bear was walking upright on his hind legs, wearing a fancy top hat and a blue bow tie.

Pascal waddled over to join Ethan and Amelia just as the dragons padded over beside them. The huge furry polar bear turned and caught sight of their little party. He lifted his black hat and waved it in greeting. Ethan waved back.

As the bear continued on his way, the door of the nearest cottage opened and out walked a very short little man. When Amelia took steps towards the house, Ethan followed.

The little man had a long, crooked nose, fat lips, and tall, pointy ears. He was shorter than Ethan, and wore smart black trousers with a green shirt and grey waistcoat. He appeared to be in a hurry. After a quick glance in their direction, he scurried away.

"There are lots of goblins," Pascal said. "And they always seem to be in a hurry."

"Oh, no," Enzo said with a sigh. When Ethan turned, he expected Enzo to tell him something about the goblins. But Enzo was flinging his head around and groaning.

"What's wrong?" Amelia asked.

"Stop it!" Enzo didn't seem to be talking to

them, but Ethan didn't have any idea who he was talking to.

"Leave him alone!" Pascal shouted. "You're always such a tease, Jojo. You'll get him in trouble again if you don't stop."

Erla took steps away from Enzo and laughed.

"Get away," Enzo growled, whipping his head from side to side. "I mean it!"

Suddenly, Ethan noticed something flying around near Enzo's scaly snout. It was the size of a small bird and moved around so fast it was hard to see.

Amelia gasped and put her hands to her face in delight. "It's the fairy!"

CHAPTER FIFTEEN
JOJO THE FAIRY

Enzo's face began to twitch. The fairy stopped in front of his snout, her delicate wings fluttering effortlessly. She wasn't dressed how Ethan would imagine a fairy to dress. There was no dress or tutu. Instead, she wore jeans with rips in them and a silver T-shirt.

As his head drew back, Enzo twitched some more. Then he let out an almighty sneeze accompanied by a ball of fire which shot into the sky.

Erla continued to laugh, and even Pascal had a small smile on his face. Nearby, a few windows flew open and goblins peered out.

"No breathing fire!" a woman shouted from an upstairs window. "You'll burn us all down."

"Sorry," Enzo shouted. "It won't happen again."

In a panic, Ethan's eyes darted around, searching out the fairy. She'd been right in the way of the fireball.

A tinkling laugh caught his attention and he spotted her standing casually on Enzo's shoulder.

"Every time!" Enzo said, shaking his head. "When will you stop playing that silly trick on me?"

"When it stops being funny," she replied with a grin.

"Wow!" Amelia moved for a closer look at the tiny, winged creature.

Jojo caught her staring and flew over to her. "Hold out your hand," she demanded. Amelia held her arm out. The fairy landed in the centre of Amelia's palm. "I'm Jojo," she said with her hands on her hips. "Who are you?"

"I'm Amelia. And this is Ethan."

"It's nice to meet you both," Jojo said. "I hope you like fun and adventures."

"I do!" Amelia said excitedly. "Adventures are my favourite thing ever."

"Tricks and games are my favourite," Jojo said. "But adventures are fun too. What kind of an adventure shall we have today?"

"I'd like you to tell me where my fishing rod is," Pascal said crossly.

"I told you I don't know." She screwed her face up into a frown. "Don't blame me because you can't look after your things!"

"I look after my things perfectly well," Pascal insisted, flapping his flippers.

Jojo stuck her tongue out at him then turned to Amelia and Ethan.

"Who wants to go for a swim in the lake?" she asked.

"We don't have swimsuits," Ethan said.

"You don't need swimsuits," Erla said, already setting off in the direction of the lake. "You can swim in your clothes."

"I don't want to get my clothes wet," Ethan said. "Especially not when it's so cold."

"You won't get wet," Pascal said loudly, waddling after Erla.

"Of course we'll get wet if we go swimming!" Ethan said.

Jojo giggled. "How on earth will you get wet in the lake?" she asked, then fluttered her wings and took off after the others. Ethan felt very confused as he walked behind them with Amelia.

"We'll get wet in the water, of course," he said.

The cheeky fairy fluttered around Ethan's head, giggling as she went. "You're very silly," she said. "The water in the lake isn't wet."

CHAPTER SIXTEEN
TIME FOR A SWIM

It was the most remarkable thing. Ethan pulled his hand from the lake and touched it to his face. The water felt wet when he put his hand in it, just like ordinary water. But as he moved his hand away, it was immediately dry. Amelia took her shoes and socks off and walked into the water from the small pebble beach. She walked straight back out of the water, then laughed and shook her feet. Ethan winced, expecting water to spray over him, but there was nothing. Not even one drop.

Amelia's whole body shook as she laughed. Then she went back into the water. This time she didn't stop but waded all the way in.

"Be careful," Ethan called. "Are you a strong swimmer?"

"I don't think I need to be!" she shouted. Her feet popped out of the water as she lay on her back. "I float."

"Of course you float!" Jojo flew around her and then landed so she was standing on the surface of the water. "Come on in!" she called to the rest of them on the shore.

"No!" Enzo said. "Dragons aren't made for water."

Erla lay at the water's edge with her front claws dipped in the water. "That's far enough for me."

Ethan waded cautiously into the lake. "Are you coming?" he asked Pascal.

"I don't like to swim," he said, shaking his head. "I'll wait here. Don't go too far!"

The water was almost up to Ethan's waist. He ran his hand along the surface. Wonderful colours from the bright twinkly sky reflected beautifully. Across the lake, near the snow-covered houses, a number of penguins and polar bears were swimming. Some penguins were even sliding down the hill at the other side of the lake and splashing into the water.

"That looks like fun," Amelia said as she watched the penguins.

"You should swim over and join them," Jojo

said. "We're the only ones at this end of the lake, because it's the no-fun zone."

"It is a bit boring," Amelia agreed. "And there is no one else here."

"No!" Enzo shouted. "The fairy's full of mischief. You'll have to learn to ignore her. Stay at this side of the lake."

"It really does look like fun, though." Amelia turned onto her front and began to swim breaststroke across the lake.

"Come back!" Enzo called. Beside him, Erla chuckled lightly.

Unsure of what to do, Ethan followed Amelia. Part of him wanted to listen to Enzo and stay where they were, but another part of him wanted to go and play with the penguins. As Ethan and Amelia swam side by side, Jojo flew just above the water, encouraging them on with shouts and cheers.

They were about halfway across the lake when Amelia shuddered. Ethan felt the water turning colder.

"Let's go back," Amelia said, swimming back the way they'd come. Jojo hovered above them, holding her stomach as she let out shrieks of delight.

After swimming a little way, they were back in the wonderfully warm water.

"What happened to the water?" Amelia shouted.

"The penguins' side of the lake is cold!" Jojo squealed. "It gets colder and colder the further you go!"

"Why didn't you tell us?" Amelia said angrily.

"You're so mean," Ethan said to Jojo. She

reminded him of the kids on his street who said unkind things. "That was a nasty trick."

"I bet it was you who took Pascal's fishing rod too," Amelia said.

Jojo tapped her feet on the surface of the water then twirled around looking very pleased with herself. "I hid it somewhere Pascal will never find it," she said with a naughty grin.

"Hey!" Ethan called as she pushed off from the water and flew away. "Come back and tell us where it is!"

It was too late – the fairy had disappeared.

CHAPTER SEVENTEEN
FISHING ROD

"We have to find it," Amelia said, looking at Ethan.

"It could be anywhere," Ethan replied. How were they supposed to know where to look?

Amelia wrinkled her forehead and looked to be deep in thought. "Jojo said it's somewhere Pascal will never find it. That means it's somewhere Pascal never goes."

"Like in the water!" Ethan said excitedly. "If it was in the lake, Pascal would never find it because he doesn't like to swim."

"Yes!" Amelia said, looking all around them. "I bet you're right."

"But if it sank to the bottom of the lake, we'll never find it," Ethan said.

"Luckily for us nothing sinks in this lake!" Amelia reminded him.

"I forgot about that," Ethan said, then joined Amelia in looking around them.

"Look!" Ethan said after a moment. He pointed to something bobbing on the water a little way from them.

"That's it!" Amelia cried. She set off swimming in that direction, then stopped abruptly. "It's over in the cold water."

Ethan shivered at the thought of it.

"Maybe we can tell Pascal where it is and he can send one of his penguin friends to get it," Amelia said. "I don't like swimming in the cold water."

Ethan didn't want to venture over there either, but he wanted to get the fishing rod for Pascal.

"We could go together," he said to Amelia. He felt much braver with her around and he was sure they could manage it if they worked together. "We'll swim really fast, grab the fishing rod, then swim back."

Amelia took a deep breath. "Okay," she said. "I suppose we can give it a try."

Ethan counted back from three, then they set off, kicking their legs as quickly as they could.

"Hurry!" Amelia said, kicking harder.

"I've got it," Ethan said, snatching at the thin rod floating on the water.

They each clung to an end of the fishing rod as they swam back.

"We made it!" Amelia cheered as they reached the warm water.

Ethan was happy to be back in the warmth. He looked at Amelia and they both began to laugh.

"Pascal will be so happy!" Ethan said.

"Come on," Amelia said. "Let's go and show him."

They swam as fast as they could back to the shore.

"Look what we found!" Ethan called, holding up the fishing rod as they walked out of the water.

"Oh my goodness!" Pascal jumped up and down excitedly. "My fishing rod!"

"You were right," Amelia said. "Jojo had hidden it - in the middle of the lake."

"Oh, that pesky little fairy!" Pascal said. "I'm so happy you found it. Thank you!"

"You're welcome," Ethan said, feeling proud of himself as he handed it back.

"Children are always good at finding things," Enzo said. He stood and stretched his wings. "I'm afraid it's time to go."

"I don't want to go home," Amelia said sadly.

"Ethan's dad will be back soon," Enzo reminded them.

Ethan realised he'd been too busy having fun to worry about getting home before his dad. It was much more exciting going on an adventure with Amelia instead of alone.

"Can we come back another day?" Ethan asked.

"Yes!" Pascal said. "You have to come back to see the stars fall. It's the most fantastic thing you'll ever see."

"The stars fall out of the sky?" Amelia asked in amazement.

"Of course," Erla said. "When the sky gets full, they all fall."

"I don't understand," Amelia said.

Ethan was confused by it too. "What's it like?" he wondered aloud. "Is it like shooting stars zooming across the sky? Do all the stars fall at once?" He gazed up at the wonderful colours which twinkled overhead.

"You'll have to wait and see." Enzo glanced up at the sky. "It is getting quite full. Maybe the next time you come it will be completely full and you'll get to see it. But now we need to go," he said impatiently. "Hurry!"

Ethan and Amelia walked back towards the hill with the rest of their little group. When they'd whizzed down it had been a very quick trip. Ethan wasn't sure how they would get back up in a hurry.

Perhaps they could fly up on the dragons. But how on earth would Pascal get up?

CHAPTER EIGHTEEN
BACK UP THE HILL

"Come along now!" Pascal called. He didn't go in the direction they'd come down to the village. The path he led them on snaked around to the side of the hill. It was almost impossible to see until they reached it, but at the side of the hill the ground was moving. It was just like the moving ice staircase in Pascal's house, but much higher, stretching all the way up the hill. And it wasn't ice but soft, moss-covered steps.

Pascal hopped onto the escalator and wobbled for a moment before finding his balance.

"Are you going to fly up?" Amelia asked the dragons.

"No," Erla replied as she began trudging up

the steep hill with Enzo. "The villagers don't like it if we fly too close to the houses. Things get blown around."

The hill was huge, and the escalator moved quite fast. Ethan was about to step on, then he hesitated. What if he fell halfway up and tumbled all the way down the hill?

Amelia slipped her hand into his. When she took a step onto the moving stairs, he did the same.

"It's pretty high, isn't it?" she said.

Ethan only nodded. He didn't really want to hold a girl's hand, but he was scared that if he let go, he'd start to wobble.

"It might feel safer if we sit down," Amelia said.

She was right; they sat side by side on the step and Ethan felt much more secure.

"Thanks, Amelia," he whispered.

She gave him the widest grin he'd ever seen. "Most kids call me Vampire Girl!"

"That's stupid," he said.

She nodded slowly. "I know."

Ethan gazed all around as they moved smoothly up the hill.

"I wish we could stay for longer," he said. "I think there's lots more to explore."

"We'll come another day." Amelia drummed her fingers on her jeans. "If you'll let me come with you? The magic dragons are yours."

"I won't come without you," he said, smiling at her. Having Amelia there with him had been much more fun. It still puzzled him that the magic had worked for her too. "I thought the magic only worked because I was afraid and wanted to be somewhere else," he said. "I thought that was why I ended up in Steorra, but I'm not sure why it worked for you too."

Amelia stared out over the village. "I was scared too," she said quietly.

"You? Scared?" Ethan couldn't believe it.

"I was nervous about being at your house," she said. "I thought you didn't like me and I didn't know what to do or talk about so I didn't really want to be there."

Ethan stared at her. He'd always thought she wasn't scared of anything. She was so loud and confident.

"I'm glad you came," he said, smiling at her.

"Me too!" Her eyes sparkled and she turned to look behind them. "Almost at the top."

She took his hand again as they stood up. This time he didn't mind and kept hold as they jumped off the top of the escalator at exactly the same time.

"We're late," Enzo said, looking anxious. "We'll need to fly from here. Climb on..." He and Erla lowered their chests to the ground, and Ethan and Amelia called goodbye to Pascal as they climbed up.

They were in the air immediately. It was hard not to smile when Amelia called out in delight. She spread her arms out wide and the wind blew her dark hair out behind her.

They soared through the clouds, and down into the swirls of colour. Then the magic disappeared, and Ethan and Amelia were back in his dull bedroom, staring at each other.

"Hello?" his dad's voice rang out from downstairs. "Ethan?"

"We're up here!" he called back.

When he moved towards the stairs, Amelia put a hand on his arm to stop him. "Promise we'll go back?" she said.

He nodded a solemn promise. "Definitely."

Together, they thundered down the stairs where his dad was taking off his shoes. "Did you have fun?" he asked.

"Yes!" Amelia said. "Lots of fun."

"That's good to hear." Ethan's dad frowned

and plucked a blade of grass from Ethan's hair. "Whatever have you been up to?"

"We went outside for a while," Ethan said weakly.

When Amelia uncurled her fist to reveal the orange dragon, Ethan realised he was still holding his too.

"We took the dragons out for an adventure!" Amelia said.

"In the garden," Ethan said quickly. "Just playing around."

"That's great," his dad said. "The fresh air is good for you. I've got some good news for you too – I've taken the day off work tomorrow! I thought we could take the train to the seaside. What do you think?"

"Brilliant!" Ethan said. A day out with his dad would be so much fun. But he caught the disappointment on Amelia's face. "Can Amelia come to play again the day after?" he asked.

His dad looked surprised. "Of course. If she wants to?"

"I'd love to," Amelia said, beaming at Ethan.

When Ethan walked Amelia to the door, she surprised him by giving him a hug. Then she pushed the orange dragon into his hand.

"I can't wait for our next adventure," she whispered. "Do you think next time we're in Steorra we'll get to see the stars fall?"

"I hope so," Ethan said.

They called goodbye to each other as Amelia stepped outside. Ethan moved into the living room and stood in the window, watching her hurry home.

"It's nice you made a friend," his dad said.

"Yes." Ethan beamed as he watched Amelia

arrive at her front door. She turned to wave and he waved back. It felt fantastic to have a friend to spend the holidays with.

So far, the summer holidays were far more exciting than he'd expected. And he had a feeling there were more adventures to come...

Don't miss the next book in the
Land of Stars series…

In a magical land called Steorra, the bright blue
sky is filling with stars. No one knows exactly
when they'll fall, but Ethan and Amelia are
determined to be there when they do.

*Join the latest exciting adventure in the wonderful
land of stars!*

ABOUT THE AUTHOR

Hannah spent most of her career working in childcare. Feeling like a change, she began writing and publishing books for grown-ups under her real name, Hannah Ellis.

In a bid to get attention from her young sons, she decided to give children's books a try! Writing about dragons and talking animals was a big change from writing romantic comedies, but she enjoyed it very much.

Sparks was Hannah's Mum's childhood nick-name and seemed like a fitting name for her children's books.

ABOUT THE ILLUSTRATOR

Katherine Newton works in various creative disciplines. Her themes and projects range from architecture, design, illustration, installation, video and music. The design and process-es overlap in many projects.

If you would like to see more of Katherine's work please visit her website:

www.kpunktnewton.com

Made in the USA
Las Vegas, NV
13 April 2024